STO ✓

SuAn

Su An

by DORIS JOHNSON

Illustrated by *Leonard Weisgard*

FOLLETT PUBLISHING COMPANY
Chicago *New York*

Also by Doris Johnson
A CLOUD OF SUMMER AND
OTHER NEW HAIKU

Library of Congress Catalog Card Number: 68-13787

First Printing   J

T/L 8370

H 1795457

To the daughters of Jo
and their mother

Through the airplane door I step.
I walk down the little stairs.
O! The wind is a tiger
switching his tail
and roaring in my ears.
He tugs at my hair.
It would please him also to have
      my sweater,
but I pull it tight around me.

I put one foot on the ground of
        America.
Then the other.
A strangeness fills the inside of me.
My heart wishes to be once more in
        Korea.
My head says, "You are lucky
to be a chosen child, Su An."
"Not so!" my heart answers.
"Will you not look again upon
        your mother's face?
Ah, Su An, I break in sadness."

My memory is like a picture
    that moves.
My mother's eyes are like two ponds
    at night in which
the moon swims. But they
    do not spill their tears.
Her voice is like the soft song of a
    bamboo flute
and the steady presence of stones
    in a garden.
"Peace, little Su An," the
    picture speaks.
"I must go away,
so I leave you here with Madame Kim.
She will take good care of you."
My mother's lips are like blossoms
    trembling in a soft breeze.
"My heart will always be with you,"
    she whispers.
"I promise."

Her kiss brushes my cheek lightly
    as a dragonfly's wing.
And she is gone.

11

For many seasons I do not speak.
I do not smile.
I do not frown.
I only wait.

Madame Kim is kind.
"Su An," she says,
"your mother would have returned
    had she been able.
But as the snow of winter melts
    in the summer sun,
so does the past depart.
Today is the day we must consider —
    and tomorrow.
Think of the coming day of happiness
when you will go to a new father
    and mother!"
I want no new mother.
I want no mother but my own.
A gray cloud descends upon my heart.

Now America burns beneath my feet.
The tiger wind roars.
Above the roar, Madame Kim calls,
"Come, children. Your new parents
    wait!"
"No! No! No!" my heart cries. "No!"
And while the others huddle,
I turn to run away.

The crooked handle of Madame Kim's
    umbrella reaches out.
It clutches my shoulder.
My heart grows angry.
"Honorable Lady of the orphanage,
O daughter of a crow," it pounds.
"You are cold as snow and hard as ice.
You have brought Su An across the sea
and lost her to her mother forever!"
Madame Kim hands her name
    papers to Nurse Chi.
She removes the crook and drops it
    over her arm.
She takes my hand and says,
"Enough of stubbornness!"
She pushes holes in the crowd
and pulls me through.
My heart weeps.
"Hush, Su An," commands my head.
"The lady knows best.
Trust her."

A door of glass opens and closes.
The tiger wind is left behind.
There are throngs of people.
They are giants —
Pale, smiling giants with big noses
    and hissing speech.
"Mother!" calls my head.
"Mother!" sobs my heart.
"O little mother of the golden skin
    and moonlit eyes."
On sticks of straw that once were legs,
I run and slip and slide.

Not once do Madame Kim's footsteps
    falter until now.
They slow. They stop.
She releases my hand.
"Greet your new parents, child,"
    she says,
and nudges me forward.
I must do what I must do!
My head bows low.
I stare at the feet of my new parents.
My father has the feet of a giant,
my mother, the feet of a doll.
I dare not raise my eyes.

"Su An."

It is the song of a bamboo flute.

"Su An."

There is a rush of fragrance.

My mother kneels.

With her fingertips, she lifts my face.

I see two ponds at night with the
    moon swimming in them.

She smiles and places a little doll
    in my hand.

It wears a happy face,

and its hair is black like mine
    and shiny.

"Don't be afraid, Su An." My new
    mother speaks.
Her voice is the steady presence
    of stones in a garden.
"Your father and I love you and want
    to take care of you.
We will have much happiness together.
I promise."

I hear the sound of my own voice.
"O-mon-i," it cries. "O-mon-i!"
With a kiss light as a dragonfly's
    wing,
my mother brushes away the tear that
    spills down my cheek.

I smile.

30

DORIS JOHNSON's interest in the Orient has led to a knowledge of its literature and a deep compassion for its war orphans. Her first book, *A Cloud of Summer* (1967) is a collection of new haiku. Mrs. Johnson, her husband, and son now live in Coquille, Oregon.

LEONARD WEISGARD has written thirteen books for children and illustrated over two hundred. In 1947, he was awarded the Caldecott Medal for *The Little Island* by Golden MacDonald. He has also designed sets and costumes for ballet. His paintings have been used on UNICEF greeting cards, and his artwork has been displayed throughout the Soviet Union and Middle Europe under the aegis of the United States Government.